D1467343

EVERYBODY
LAUGHS

Illustrations by Em is a small creative
business founded and ran by Emily Barnes.
She publishes children's books, comics and
illustrations, does custom portraits, design
work, and sells uniquely designed products
in her online shop. Her brand values
humor, optimism, imagination, and a
ravenous pursuit of adventure to challenge
complacency and its rootin' tootin'
sidekick, the status quo.

illustrationsbyem.com

EVERYBODY LAUGHS

by
EMILY BARNES

AN ILLUSTRATIONS by Em
PUBLICATION

Once upon a time
in a future not far away,
there lived a girl named Zoey
who always had friends to play.

She didn't feel a smidge lonely.
How could she? She was not alone.

School, walking home, and free time,
she was never on her own.

One day as Zoey was walking home
with her friends Ally and Kate,
she noticed Lulu trailing behind them.

Lulu— their new classmate.

Lulu was not like other children
with three eyes
and skin bright green!

Nobody wanted to include her,
because she was not a human being.

"I know she's not human,"
Zoey told her mom and dad.

"But why doesn't she try to make friends?
Being alone all the time is sad."

They told Zoey Lulu's story:
Her family immigrated
from Mars!

"Imagine being in her shoes," they said.
"Moving from a different world to ours."

Zoey tried to imagine,

but gave up and fell asleep.

She sank into dreamland,
and she sank

deep

deep

deep.

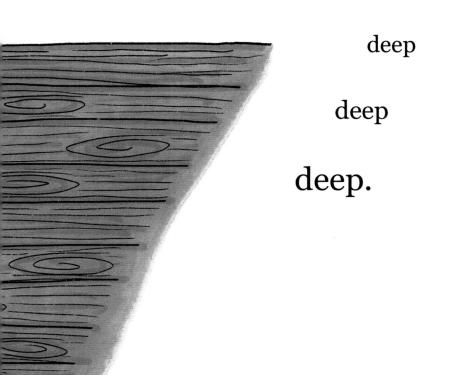

Suddenly Zoey woke
and her heart pounded with fright,
because when she looked out her window
there wasn't a human in sight!

All she saw was Lulu
and kids that looked
just the same.

Martians, martians, martians!
Swinging and playing games.

Slowly Zoey dressed
and bravely went outside,
and felt a new feeling
that wounded her pride.

Nobody would talk to her!
Two were swinging on a tree.
Too busy laughing with each other
to look, notice, or see.

"Lulu!" Zoey called.

She tried to get her to glance.

Even she wouldn't notice

—wouldn't give her a chance.

Zoey closed her eyes in sadness,
and then her world started to spin!

Twirling

swirling

whirling, until...

Ka-thump!
It was her bedroom
she was in.

She sat in shock for a moment.

It had all just been a dream!

She smiled out her window.

A normal day did gleam.

Sighing loudly in relief,

her stomach tossed and turned in guilt.

She felt bad for ignoring Lulu

now that she knew how bad it felt.

As she changed out of her pajamas,
she decided hard and true:

"At school, I'll be nice to Lulu.
It's something I must do."

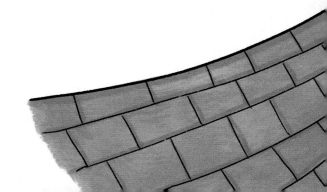

But today was Saturday,
so she raced down the street.

It was sunny on a weekend,
and her friends had planned to meet.

She reached the park and saw her friends
leaning on the trees,
but her eyes caught Lulu sitting behind them.

Zoey's feet did freeze.

"I want to play with my friends," she thought.

"Not try and meet someone new—

but what of the lesson my scary dream taught?

Yes, this is something I must do."

Zoey walked towards Lulu.
Her hands fluttered with nerves,
and when Lulu saw her coming,
her own thoughts started to swerve.

"What does she want?"
Lulu wondered with a sigh,
but when Zoey finally got there
Lulu was too shy to ask why.

'Hi!" Zoey said.

"Zoey is my name.

I know this is random,

but do you want to play a game?"

"I'm Lulu," was her response.

"I just moved here from Mars.

Okay, let's see how long we can dangle

on the monkey bars."

They walked to the playground
and Ally and Kate also came.
Together they laughed, laughed, laughed...

...everybody's laugh was just the same.

For more free downloadable coloring pages
from *Everybody Laughs* AND MORE, go to
illustrationsbyem.com

@illustrationsbyem

 Illustrations by Em

ABOUT THE AUTHOR & ARTIST

Emily Barnes founded Illustrations by Em in 2018, two years after graduating with a Bachelor's in English and writing from Portland State University. She strives to cultivate a space that stretches the imagination, shares positivity and creativity, and provides a lifestyle and career that is challenging, ever - evolving, and independent.